D0354118

Yann Andrea Steiner

Yann Andrea Steiner

A Memoir

Marguerite Duras

*Translated from the French
by Barbara Bray*

Charles Scribner's Sons
New York

Maxwell Macmillan Canada
Toronto

Maxwell Macmillan International
New York Oxford Singapore Sydney

English translation copyright © 1993 by Macmillan Publishing Company,
a division of Macmillan, Inc.
Originally published as *Yann Andréa Steiner* by P.O.L, Paris, in 1992.
Copyright © 1992 by P.O.L

All rights reserved. No part of this book may be reproduced or transmitted in
any form or by any means, electronic or mechanical, including photocopying,
recording, or by any information storage and retrieval system, without
permission in writing from the Publisher.

Charles Scribner's Sons
Macmillan Publishing Company
866 Third Avenue
New York, NY 10022

Maxwell Macmillan Canada, Inc.
1200 Eglinton Avenue East
Suite 200
Don Mills, Ontario M3C 3N1

Macmillan Publishing Company is part of the Maxwell Communication
Group of Companies.

Library of Congress Cataloging-in-Publication Data
Duras, Marguerite.
  [Yann Andréa Steiner. English]
  Yann Andrea Steiner : a memoir /Marguerite Duras : translated
from the French by Barbara Bray.
    p. cm.
  ISBN 0-684-19590-9
I. Title.
PQ2607.U8245T3613   1993
843'.912—dc20   93-15599   CIP

Macmillan books are available at special discounts for bulk purchases for
sales promotions, premiums, fund-raising, or educational use. For details,
contact: Special Sales Director, Macmillan Publishing Company,
866 Third Avenue, New York, NY 10022

10 9 8 7 6 5 4 3 2 1

Printed in the United States of America

Book Design by Ellen R. Sasahara

Yann Andrea Steiner

Before everything, before the story told here began, *India Song* was shown at an art cinema in the large town where you lived. After the film there was a debate in which you took part. Then after the debate we went to a bar with the young student teachers, of whom you were one. It was you who reminded me afterwards, long afterwards, about the bar, which was pleasant and quite smart; you also reminded me I'd had a couple of whiskeys there that evening. I had no recollection of the whiskeys, nor of you, nor of the other young student teachers, nor of the place. I did remember, or rather had the impression, that you'd walked me back to the parking lot by the cinema where I'd left my car. I still had the old Renault 16 that I was so fond of and that I still drove fast even then, after my health had been affected by drinking. You asked me if I had lovers. I said not any more, as a matter of fact. You asked me how fast I drove at night.

I said a hundred and forty kilometers an hour. The same as anyone else with a Renault 16. It was terrific, I said.

After that evening you started writing me letters. Lots of them. Sometimes one a day. They were very short letters, notes almost, yes, appeals almost, cries rising up from somewhere unbearable, deadly, a kind of desert. They were unmistakably beautiful.

I didn't reply.
But I kept all the letters.
At the top of every page was the place where it had been written, and the time or the weather. Sunshine or Rain. Or Cold. Or Alone.

And then you didn't write for a long time. A month perhaps. I can't remember how long it lasted.

So then in the void you'd left, the absence of letters, the absence of cries, *I* wrote to *you* to find out
why you weren't writing any more, why, why all of a
sudden you'd stopped, as if something had forcibly
prevented you, death for example.

This is the letter I wrote you:

Yann Andrea, this summer I met someone you
know, Jean-Pierre Ceton. We talked about you, I'd
had no way of knowing you knew each other. And
then there was your note under my door in Paris after
The Navire Night. I tried to phone you, but I couldn't
find your number. And then there was your January
letter. I was back in the hospital, ill again with I can't
quite remember what. They said I'd been poisoned by
some new medication, antidepressants so-called.
Always the same old story. It was nothing, there was
nothing wrong with my heart. I didn't even feel sad, I
was just at the end of something, that's all. I was still
drinking—yes, in the winter, in the evening. For years
I'd been telling my friends not to come for the week-
end any more, I lived all by myself in the house at

Neauphle, big enough to hold ten people. Alone in fourteen rooms. You get used to the echoes. So there you are. I did write to you once to tell you I'd just finished the film called *Son Nom de Venise dans Calcutta désert.* I don't really remember what I told you about it, probably that I adored it, as I do almost all my films. You didn't answer. And then there were the poems you sent me. I thought some of them very fine, some less so, but I didn't know how to tell you. That was it. Yes. I didn't know how to say it was your letters that were your poems. Your letters are beautiful, the most beautiful in my whole life, it seemed to me—so beautiful they hurt. And then today I wanted to talk to you. I'm still only convalescent, but I'm writing. Working. I think the second *Aurélia Steiner* was written for you.

It seemed to me that letter didn't call for an answer either. I was just telling you how I was getting on. I remember another letter, desolate and incoherent, written when I was depressed by some problem that had cropped up, some new loneliness, recent and unexpected. For a long while I knew almost nothing about that letter, I wasn't even sure I'd written it that summer, the summer you came into my life. And I wasn't sure where I'd written it, either. I didn't think it was at that place by the sea, but I couldn't remember where else it might be. It was a good while later that I thought I could remember the shape of my room surrounding the letter, the black marble fireplace and the mirror right in front of me. I wondered at the time whether or not I ought to send it. I wasn't sure I had sent it until you told me you'd had a letter like that from me two years before.

I can't recall seeing that letter again. You talked about it often. You were very struck by it. You said it was fantastic, that it told everything about my life and work without ever openly referring to my life itself. There was a kind of indifference, a kind of abstraction about it that frightened you. And you said it *was* from Taormina I'd sent it. But dated from Paris, five days before.

Years later we lost it, that long letter of mine. You said you'd put it away in a certain chest of drawers in the apartment in Trouville, and I must have taken it out again. But the day you said that, you couldn't remember anything about what went on in the apartment or anywhere else. You were always out in the gardens and the bars of the big hotels in Mont-Canisy, on the lookout for handsome barmen from Buenos Aires and Santiago who'd been taken on for the summer. And I was lost in the sexual labyrinth of *Blue Eyes, Black Hair.* It was a long time after I'd spoken of our story in that book that I found the letter in the chest of drawers. It must have been there all the time.

Two days after that letter, the one that was lost and found again, you phoned me here, at Roches Noires, to say you were coming to see me.

Your voice on the phone was slightly different, as if apprehensive, shy. I didn't recognize it. It was. . .I don't know how to put it. . .yes, that's it, it was the voice of your letters, which I'd been creating in my imagination just when you phoned.

You said, "I'm coming."

I asked why.

You said, "For us to get to know one another."

At that time in my life it was a terrifying thing, someone coming to see me like that, from a long way away. Admittedly I've never talked, never, about how lonely I was at that time. After *The Ravishing of Lol V. Stein* and at the time of *Blue Moon*, and *Love*, and *The Vice-Consul*. That was the deepest loneliness I ever experienced in my life, but the happiest, too. I didn't see it as loneliness—rather as an opportunity to attain a crucial and hitherto unknown freedom. I used to eat at the Central: some prawns and a Mont Blanc, always the same. I didn't go swimming. The sea was as crowded as the town. I only went in during the evening when my friends Henry Chatelain and Serge Derumier were there.

You told me afterwards that you'd rung me several days running, before, but I wasn't in. Later on I told you why, reminded you I'd had to go to the Taormina film festival, where I'd arranged to meet Benoît Jacquot, a very dear friend of mine. But I'd had to be back soon because, as you knew, I was writing a weekly column about the summer of 1980 for *Libération*.

I asked again, "What are you coming for?"

You said, "To talk to you about Theodora Kats."

I said I'd abandoned the book about Theodora Kats after thinking for years I could write it. I said I'd hidden it for ever, for the eternity of my own death, in a Jewish place, a grave I regarded as sacrosanct—vast, bottomless and forbidden to traitors, to the living dead of the ultimate treachery.

I asked when you were coming. You said, "Tomorrow morning. The bus gets in at ten-thirty and I'll be at your place by eleven."

I waited for you on the balcony outside my bedroom. You walked across the courtyard of the Résidence des Roches Noires.

I'd forgotten the man in *India Song*.

You were a sort of tall, thin Breton and struck me as elegant, though very unobtrusively and unconsciously—one can always tell. You walked along without looking at the Résidence building. Without looking in my direction at all. You had a big wooden umbrella, a sort of Chinese sunshade made of glazed cotton. Not many young men carried one of those in the 1980s. You also had a minimal amount of luggage. A black canvas bag.

You walked across the courtyard, by the hedge, then turned off towards the sea and disappeared into the entrance hall of the apartment building without once looking up at me.

So it happened at eleven o'clock in the morning, at the beginning of July.

It was the summer of 1980. The summer of wind and rain. The summer of Gdansk. Of the little boy who wept. Of the girl, the young camp counselor. And of our affair, our story. It was the first summer of the story told here, of the affair between the young Yann Andrea Steiner and the woman who wrote books and who was old, old and as alone as he was in that summer almost as vast as Europe itself.

I'd told you how to find my apartment. The floor, the corridor, the door.

You never went back to the city of Caen. It happened in July 1980. Twelve years ago. And you still live here in this apartment for six months every year, the six months' annual vacation I've taken ever since that two-year illness of mine. That horrific coma. A few days before they were going to "terminate" me, on the unanimous decision of the doctors in the section of the hospital I was being treated in, I opened my eyes. I looked. The people, the room. They were all there—

I was told about it later. I looked at those motionless people in white coats, smiling at me in a kind of madness, of crazy, silent joy. I didn't recognize their faces, but I did recognize their shapes as belonging to human beings, not to walls or bits of equipment but to people with eyes, looking at me. And then I shut my eyes again. And opened them again so as to see the people again. With, so I was told, an amused smile in my eyes.

There was a silence.

Then came the knocks at the door and then your voice, "It's me. It's Yann." I didn't answer. The knocks were very, very soft, as if everyone around you were asleep—in the Résidence and in the town, on the beach and on the sea, and in all the hotel rooms there ever were on summer mornings by the sea.

Once more I didn't open right away. I still waited. You said again, "It's me. Yann." As softly and calmly as before. I still waited. I didn't make a sound. For ten years I'd been living in a strict, almost monastic solitude, with Anne-Marie Stretter, with the French Vice-

Consul in Lahore and with her, the Queen of the Ganges, the beggar woman on the Tea Road, the queen of my childhood.

I opened the door.

You never know a story until it's written. Until the circumstances that made the author write it have been removed. And above all until its past has been lopped off, together with its body and your face and your voice, and it becomes inevitable, fated. I mean until, set down in a book, it becomes external, far off, separate from and lost for all eternity to its author.

And then there was the door closing on you and on me. On the new body, tall and thin.

And then there was the voice. The incredibly gentle voice. Distant. Regal. It was the voice of your letter, and of my life.

We talked for hours.

All the time about books. All the time, for several hours. You talked about Roland Barthes. I reminded you what I thought of him. I told you I'd give all Roland Barthes' books put together for my tea roads through the forests of Burma, the red sun and the dead children of the poor women of the Ganges. But you knew that already. I also told you I just couldn't manage to read him, that for me Roland Barthes stood for false writing, and it was this falseness that had killed him. I told you later on that one day at my place he had kindly advised me to "go back" to the style of my early novels, "so simple and charming"—novels like *A Wall against the Pacific, The Little Horses of Tarquinia,* and *The Sailor from Gibraltar.* I laughed. You said we'd never talk about it again. And I guessed you'd had enough of that brilliant author.

And we talked, as we always do, about that great matter, writing. About books and more books.

It was when you started talking about books that, behind the attentive look and the lucid reasoning, I was struck by a kind of urgency you couldn't restrain, as if you had to move fast in order to be able to tell me all you'd decided to tell me, and all you'd decided not to say, too. All you wanted to tell me before . . . It suddenly became terribly, dazzlingly clear: you'd decided to meet me and then kill yourself.

Very soon that was all I could remember about you.

Much later on you talked about it, you said yes, it was probably true, adding rather obscurely, "The same as you, in a different way." You didn't say the actual word. Later on I realized that even to yourself you had to keep silent about it. About the word that was spoken in your smile: writing.

And then it was evening. I said, "You can stay here, you can sleep in my son's room." I said it looked out on the sea, the bed was made up.

And if you wanted to take a bath, you could do that, too.

And similarly if you would rather go out . . .

And similarly, if you liked, you could, say, buy a cold chicken, a tin of chestnut purée, some cream to go with it, and some fruit and cheese and bread. I said that was what I ate every day, to simplify life. And I said you could buy a bottle of wine for yourself. I said that on some days I didn't drink as much as I had. We both laughed.

No sooner had you gone out than you were back again. "Money," you said. "I haven't any left after the bus. I'd forgotten."

You ate with the appetite of a child. I didn't know then that you always did.

A long time afterwards you told me you were still hungry when we got up from the table. Even after eating up all the chestnut purée and cream without so much as noticing.

Perhaps it was that evening, with you, that I started drinking again. We drank the two half-bottles of Côtes du Rhône that you'd bought in the rue des Bains. Even though it was musty and undrinkable, we drank the two half-bottles of the wine from the rue des Bains.

The first night you slept in the room overlooking the sea. No sound came from it, any more than when I was alone. You must have been worn out with fatigue, too, after days, months, perhaps years—barren, tragic years of endurance, of wondering what to do about the future, and the agonizing years of adolescent desire and solitude like mine.

The day after you arrived you discovered the bath-tub in the main bathroom. You said you'd never seen a bathtub like that before, it was monumental, "historic." Every morning after that, as soon as you were up, you spent an hour in it. I told you you could stay there as long as you liked, I always took a shower because the bathtub scared me, probably because there were no bathtubs in the houses provided for government officials in the back of beyond I was brought up in.

Your voice. It was incredibly gentle, distant, intimidating, almost unarticulated, scarcely audible, always rather absent and uninvolved in what it was saying, separate. Even now, twelve years later, I can still hear the voice you had then. It has become part of my body. It has no image. It speaks of things that are unimportant. And it can be silent too.

We talked, you said how beautiful it was here at the Roches Noires.

Then you were silent, as if thinking out how to say what you had to tell me. You couldn't hear the growing peace that came with the darkness, a peace so deep I went out on the balcony to look at it. Every so often cars drove past the Roches Noires on the way to Honfleur or Le Havre. Le Havre was lit up, as every night, as if for some celebration, with a bare sky above, and between the sky and the Sainte-Adresse lighthouse came the black procession of tankers sailing down as usual towards the ports of France and southern Europe.

You stood up. You looked at me through the windowpanes. You were still in a state of deep abstraction.

I came back into the room.

You sat down again facing me and said, "Aren't you ever going to write the story of Theodora?"

I said I was never sure about what I was or wasn't going to write.

You didn't answer.

I said, "You're in love with Theodora."

You didn't smile, you said without pausing for breath, "Theodora is what I don't know about you, I was very young. I know all the rest. I've been waiting three years for you to write her story."

I said, "I don't really know why I can't write it."

Then I added, "Perhaps it's too difficult. There's no way of knowing."

There were tears in your eyes.

You said, "Don't tell me anything you know about her."

And then you said, "I don't know anything about her except the last few pages of *Outside*."

"So you did know how she made love to that lover."

"Yes. I knew that was how the wives of deportees made love to their husbands when they came back exhausted from the camps in the north of Nazi Germany."

I said I'd probably never finish Theodora, the book about Theodora. That it was practically certain. It was the only time in my life this had ever happened to me. The most I'd been able to do was salvage that passage from the abandoned manuscript. It was a book I couldn't write without veering off at once toward other books I'd never intended to embark on.

After that you went out on the balcony, to the balustrade overlooking the sea. I didn't hear another sound from you.

We went to bed with the moon in a dark blue sky. It was the next day that we made love.

You came to me in my bedroom. We didn't say a word. We were fueled by the childish body of Theodora Kats, that crippled body, its bright eyes, its cries to its mother before it was shot in the neck by the German soldier in charge of the camp. Afterwards you said my body was incredibly young. I've hesitated about writing that down for publication. But I hadn't

the strength not to. I write down things I don't understand, too. I leave them in my books and reread them
later and then they take on a meaning. I said people
always told me that, even the North China Lover said
the same thing, and I was only fourteen at the time, if
that. . .and we laughed. And desire came back again,
without a word, without a kiss. And after we'd made
love you spoke to me about Theodora Kats. About the
words: Theodora Kats. Even the name was shattering,
you said.

Then you asked, "So why the difficulty, all of a
sudden?"

I said, "I don't know, all I know is it might be
because of something I was told. . .that at the time
Theodora Kats was deported the crematoria didn't yet
exist. The bodies just rotted in the graves. The crematoria came later, after 1942 and the Final Solution."

You asked if that was really what had made me
abandon Theodora Kats to her fate.

I said, "Perhaps: she'd been dead a long time and
everyone had forgotten her, perhaps I had, too.
She'd been so young, twenty-three, twenty-five at
the most."

I seemed to remember she was slightly disabled. Nothing serious, just a slight limp in the left ankle.

You asked, "And have the Germans forgotten?"

"Yes. Otherwise they might have died at the mere realization that they were German, inescapably German."

"And that's what you hoped?"

"Yes. But three years after the war, time began to move—move on again. At first for them, the Germans, as always, and then for people in other countries. But not for them, the Jews, ever."

You asked me to go on talking to you about Theodora Kats, even though you did know so little about her.

So that evening I talked to you about Theodora Kats, the person I thought of as her, her again, still alive, but just after the war, the year after the war ended. I told you the hotel she was staying in was in Switzerland, that it was there, in the Valley Hotel, that she must have been living at the last, before she died. And it was to this same Swiss hotel—a square building with a fountain and statues of women bathing—they'd brought back children who'd been found dying in the Nazi camps. And all day long these children, about whom no one knew anything, were shouting and eating and laughing, and it was impossible to live there, among those small survivors. And yet it was in the Valley Hotel that Theodora Kats had been really happy, apparently.

You asked, with a gentleness that surprised me, "Were the children orphans?"

I couldn't answer. And you asked again, "Jewish?"

Probably, I said. But one mustn't ever generalize any more, I said. And yet I wept, because I was still there with those Jewish children. "Yes, Jewish," I said.

I told you how, there in the Swiss hotel, the children stole food—bread and cakes—and hid it. They hid everything. And took off all their clothes and dived into the pool around the fountain. They were mad about water. And everyone watched them. There wasn't anything else to do in that hotel. They used to hurt themselves in the concrete pool, but they were too happy to feel it. Sometimes the water was pink with their blood and had to be changed. But you couldn't stop them from doing whatever they chose.

If we tried to pat them on the cheek they would scratch us, spit at us.

A lot of them had forgotten their mother tongue, their first name, their family name, their parents. When they shouted, their shouts were all in different languages, but they understood one another. Rumor in the hotel had it that they were all from Poland, from the Vilna ghetto, once as big as a whole county.

"It was because of the children that Theodora fled from the hotel. So as to be able to go on living."

I said she *might* have fled from the hotel—but I didn't think she had.

I said Theodora was dependent on me. Ever since I'd known her, even though I hadn't written much about her, whatever happened to her had depended entirely on me.

It also seemed to me, I said, that it depended on when it was I thought about her. At night I used to think I'd seen her somewhere before. Sometimes, in the daytime, I'd think I'd met her before the war, in Paris. But then, in the morning, I wouldn't be able to remember—I might think I'd never met her, ever, anywhere.

"Did you invent the name Theodora?"

"Yes. I invented everything about that young woman—the green of her eyes, the beauty of her body, and her voice. Because I knew she'd been killed in the gas chambers. And I recognized the name when I first heard it. So I must have invented it, must have imagined it already. Perhaps I invented it so as to be able to speak of the Jews who were murdered by the Germans. A body without a name was useless."

You said, "You ought to say 'Nazis.'"

I said I'd never said "Nazis" to mean the Germans.

And I would go on calling them the Germans. I believed there were some Germans who would never get over their massacres, their gas chambers, their slaughtering of Jewish infants and their surgical experiments on Jewish boys and girls. Never.

She lived in a little room in the rue de l'Université or thereabouts. . . . She was very lonely. Her face was magnificent. She was a friend of Betty Fernandez's, too—Betty had lent her the room when the Germans came.

What I remember most is how much she, Theodora Kats, wanted to learn French well enough to write in it.

I wept. And we stopped talking. The night was almost over. I went on weeping in bed, where we'd sought refuge after talking about the children. You said, "Don't cry."

I said I couldn't help it. These tears had become a kind of duty, a vital necessity. Being able to cry my eyes out, to cry my life out, was my good fortune, I knew that. And for me, writing was like weeping. A happy book was indecent, unseemly. We ought to wear mourning as a sign of civilization, a sign that we remember every man-made death of any kind, whether it took place in prison or in war.

You asked, "What should we do with the French Nazis?"

"I don't know, any more than you do. Murder them. The French would have become murderers themselves, you know, if they'd been allowed to kill the German Nazis, pay them back. Letting them live brought disgrace on the name of France. And we still hanker after the murder we failed to commit."

I came into your arms and we wept together. Every so often we'd laugh, embarrassed by our tears. Then the tears would come back and we'd laugh again at not being able to help them.

You said, "You never met Theodora."

"Yes, I did. But in the shape of beautiful women who might have passed me in the street, or of film and theater actresses, women like that. Well-known women, some beautiful, some not, but famous and talked about. Yes, a whole race of Theodoras, everywhere. For years you could see Theodora Kats everywhere."

"Someone else knew about her . . .?"

"Yes. Betty Fernandez had heard of her. People said she'd been seen in 1942 at a German railway station, a kind of railhead for the trains transporting Jews. They found some very fine drawings of her there. She must have been dropped there by mistake—no Jewish deportees were ever picked up there to be taken to the camps at Auschwitz. People said she was alone there with the stationmaster. They also said she might just have got out at the wrong stop by mistake. Or maybe some German told her to get out there, to save her life perhaps; because of her face, so gentle and lovely; because of her youth. She collected her case and got off there without question. She must have been so determined to take that train, so beautiful, so elegant in her spotless dress that no one, not even an inspector, asked to see her ticket. The charcoal drawings all showed the same young woman in the same white clothes. Sitting under a tree, always the same one, in a corner of the garden, in a white chair always facing the station. The drawings weren't found all put away together in one part of the station. Some were on the ground in the yard outside. They were scattered about everywhere. But mostly on the ground, apparently. People might have gone to live in the station after the war, the drawings might have been looted. They were all almost the same, Theodora Kats dressed all in white, very English, white-skinned, with her hair neatly done, discreetly made up, wearing a straw hat and sitting in a canvas chair, always under the same tree, with an ordinary breakfast tray set out in front of her. She must have stayed there a long time, Theodora. She got up early and took a shower, always at the same time, then dressed and went out into the garden to have breakfast before catching the train that would one day get her out of there, out of Germany. The stationmaster used to bring her nourishing food every day. He said he waited for the train, too—they both waited for it every day without fail. Every morning of every day they used to wait for the same train, the Jews' train. And every day, after each train that went by without stopping, she would say *her* train must come now, she couldn't wait any longer. I've thought a lot about that train, always going by at the same time. I believe I may also have thought that, for Theodora Kats, that train—the train of death by beheading, the train that supplied Auschwitz with living flesh—was the train of hope.

All her life she spoke very little, Theodora. Like a lot of Englishwomen, she regarded speech as noisy and deceptive. She had chosen the silence of writing. You asked whereabouts the station was. She herself thought it was south of Krakow, toward the frontier. That godforsaken part of the world. She was English by birth, but had been raised in Belgium. She wasn't very well up on the geography of Europe. Like a lot of English people, she was interested only in the London-Paris run and the Gulf states.

You asked me if the man in charge of the station came to her while she was asleep. I thought that was what I'd written—yes, while she slept. I wasn't sure it *wasn't* the stationmaster of that station where she lived for two years during the war. Why not? And why mightn't they have been in love?—I'd thought of that too. And that that might have been the grief she died of, later on.

I hadn't tried to find out, I said. I hadn't asked that sort of thing about Theodora, but it was not impossible that they might have become lovers.

You asked me what I thought. I told you I'd never asked their names—neither the man's nor that of the young woman in white in the drawings. As soon as I heard their story I spoke the name, Theodora Kats. As I'd said, I had heard it before. And then, a few years later, other people used that name, too, for the woman in white lost in a Europe of death.

I reminded you I knew I'd met Theodora, but all my memories came through Betty Fernandez, whom I knew very well and who, as I'd said before, was young Theodora Kats's friend. I said I knew Betty Fernandez was very fond of her and admired her.

I'd never forgotten that name, that time, the white of those dresses, that innocent waiting for the train of death or love, no one knew, no one ever knew.

You said that even if I didn't know Theodora, even if I'd never met her, I must tell you what *I* thought might have happened to her.

I think, personally, she went back to England before the end of the war. That to begin with she worked on a well-known literary review in London. And then she married G.O., the English writer. And she wasn't very cheerful. I knew her best after she married G.O., who was a worldwide success and whom I admired enormously. But she never liked him much either as a writer or as a man.

You asked me what Theodora was like in London. I said she'd put on weight. And she didn't make love to her husband any more, she didn't want that any more, ever. She'd rather die, she said.

You said, "And was the woman in London the same as the one at the station in Germany?"

"I never tried to check. That's all I can say. But I don't think it's impossible. Something must have happened to her, after all. Even if she'd been dead something would have happened—she'd have been claimed by a family in England or some other country. But no. No one ever claimed Theodora Kats's body."

"Yet she did leave that station at some time."

"Yes. Unless she was found there after Germany was defeated—the Nazis had simply left her there at the station, just as they left the 'Politicals' in the camps, thousands of them. As for what became of her lover, no one ever found out. Not anything. But she had been there in that station. I can just see her there, still wearing her white suits freshly pressed every day, and that day spattered with her own blood."

I think what's prevented her from ever being forgotten is the white. It's the white of her dresses, the strange and excessive care she took of them, that has prevented anyone who ever heard of her from forgetting her—the white linen caps, the canvas sandals and everything, the gloves. Her story trailed around all Europe. But no one ever could be certain. No one knows even now what she was like or why she was there in that station for two years on end.

Yes, it's the white of the dresses, of the summer suits, that has made her story spread all over the world; a very English lady in spotless white, waiting for the train to the gas chambers.

For most people it's the respectable white image that survives. And for others it's the laugh.

"Or perhaps she didn't have a story at all."

"Perhaps not. Perhaps she just went out of her

mind with a quiet, lurking madness that deprived her of the will to see and know and understand. Perhaps a kind of normal madness took possession of her, of her mind and her body. As for me, I've done my best to re-create the phenomenon of the station, make it happen again. And it has happened again."

You asked me if she was dead. I said yes. And that the ceremonial of the station had happened again. She didn't want to be seen at a disadvantage—cancer had made her very thin and got the better of her bright beauty. So she rented a room in a big hotel near the hospital where she'd been treated and to which she asked to be taken later. She asked for her prettiest dress and for her face to be made up. And it was there her friends saw her for the last time—as she had been when she was alive, but dead.

It was raining.

Raining over the sea.

Over the forests, over the empty beach.

It had been raining since last night. A fine, light rain.

The summer sunshades weren't out yet. The only movement in all those acres of sand came from the children from the summer camps. They looked small to me that year, very small. Every so often the camp counselors let them loose on the beach. To save themselves from going crazy.

Here they came.

Shouting.

They liked the rain.

The sea.

They shouted louder and louder.

After an hour they were worn out. Then they were put back in their tents. They had their clothes changed, their backs rubbed so they wouldn't catch cold, they loved that, they laughed and shouted.

The counselors got them to sing a song. They sang, but raggedly. It was always the same. What they liked best was to be told stories. Anything so long as it was a story. They didn't want to sing songs.

Except one. One who just looked.

The little boy. The one with gray eyes. He came along with the others.

We asked him, "Don't you like running about?"

He shook his head. He was very silent, that child. Silent for hours sometimes.

"Why are you crying?" we asked him. He didn't answer. He didn't know.

If only everything had the grace of the boy who was crying. The grace of the sea when he looked at it.

Wasn't he happy here? He didn't answer, he shook his head vaguely as if apologizing about some small difficulty, something quite unimportant really, nothing.

And suddenly we saw.

Saw that the splendor of the sea was there, too, in the eyes of the boy looking at it.

The boy looked. Looked at everything—at the sea, at the beaches, into space. His eyes were gray. *Gray.* Like a storm, like stone, like the northern sky, the sea, the mind that is immanent in matter, in life. Gray as thought. As time. As the centuries past and to come all rolled into one. *Gray.*

Did the boy know there was someone on the beach looking after him? A dark-haired girl with eyes both sad and laughing? We didn't know. Her name was Johanna.

At one point you might have thought he'd turned to look at her. But no, he was just looking around to see where the wind was blowing from, it was so strong, so steady, so strong you'd have thought it had changed direction and was blowing from the forests, from some place unknown...you'd have thought it had left the ocean sky, here, for some place unknown belonging to another time.

Yes, that was what he was looking at, the wind. Which had fled out to sea. A great stretch, a great strand of wind flying out over the sea.

So the person looking after him was Johanna, Jeanne, a young and cheerful camp counselor. "What do you think about all the time?" she asked him. He said he didn't know. She said it was the same with her, she never knew either. Then it was his turn to look at her.

That day there was a kite in the bare sky—the sort they make in China. I wasn't quite sure but I thought I recognized the red of Chinese lacquer, the red of North China.

The boy stood there. He, too, was looking at the kite, the red shape in the sky. He was standing a little way away from the others, but not deliberately. It must always have been like that. As if he were always lagging behind the rest, though never consciously.

When the kite fell down dead the boy looked at it, then sat down on the sand to look some more, at a kite that had died.

The gulls were there, too, facing out to sea, their feathers smoothed by the wind. They stood perched on the sand, watching the confused swirling of the rain. And suddenly started to shriek—deafening, frightening. Then for no apparent reason they chased out to sea and as swiftly flew back again. Cracked, the children called them.

The children went back up the hill to their canteen. The beach slowly emptied, as it did at that time every day in the summer, the time when the children in the camps had their lunch. The girls looking after them called them in. The little boy stood up and waited for Johanna, Jeanne. Then put his hand in hers and went off with her.

One day the summer will end. Sometimes this thought comes back to me on the beach, right in the sun, through the transparency of the rollers. Sometimes it comes when summer stretches out as far as the eye can see, blindingly bright. Sometimes when it's dark, sometimes when it sheds light over everything. Or when you're not there, and I'm alone in the world.

I'd never know if one day the little boy would know there was someone here on the beach watching him. He'd turned round in my direction once or twice, but only to look at the armies of kites. Or at the wind. Or the gulls. Now he was looking at the girl, the camp counselor. He knew she'd been assigned to look after him.

That was the first time I'd seen the boy's body so close. He was thin and tall, perhaps too tall for his age. Six, he said he was.

A second kite darted crazily towards the sea and then was caught in the snares of the wind. The boy ran as if to catch up with it, but the kite fell down dead. The boy stopped and looked at the dead kite. And then walked on.

The aria from *Norma* floated out from the Résidence again. Callas, in the distance, was weeping again, mourning with the boy over the dead kite.

In the midst of the bad weather there was an hour of sunshine and the beach was suddenly wrapped in warmth. The wind had dropped and the children were told they could go swimming. The water was warm after the rain.

The girl didn't go with him, she didn't even look at him any more. She could see him without looking. The boy took off his warm jacket as if he were all alone in the world, went and put it down beside her, and made off toward the sea with the other children. He didn't say anything about the death of the second kite.

It wasn't long before he was back on the beach with her.

He was wearing a white swimsuit. He was thin. You could see his body plainly. He was too tall and seemed to be made of glass, like a windowpane—you could see already how he would turn out.

You could see the perfect proportions and joints, the long muscles. The miraculous fragility of wrists and ankles, of the bones, the folds in the neck, the legs, the hands. You could see it all already.

And the head, emerging like a tangent, a beacon, the culminating tip of a flower.

And then all of a sudden the nights were hot. And after that the days.

And the little children in the summer camps took an afternoon nap in their blue and white tents.

And the eyes of the boy who didn't speak were shut, and there was nothing to distinguish him from the other children.

And the young camp counselor came up close to him. And he opened his eyes. "Were you asleep?" The usual apologetic smile, and he didn't answer. "Don't you know when you're asleep?" He smiled again, and said not really.

"How old are you?" "Six and a half," he said. The girl's lips quivered. "May I give you a kiss?" He smiled, yes. She put her arms around him and kissed his hair, his eyes. Then she withdrew her arms and lips from the child's body. There were tears in her eyes, as

the child saw, too. He was used to it, he knew he
sometimes made people who looked at him cry. But he
was used to it. And he talked about the past few days,
and said he missed the storms and the big waves and
the rain.

"Will they come back?" he asked.

"They always do," said the girl.

"Every day?" asked the child.

"Who knows?" said the girl.

Sometimes I see you and don't know you at all, not at all. I see you far away from this beach, somewhere else, a long way away, sometimes in another country. The memory of you is already there even when you're present, but already I can't remember your hands. It's as if I'd never seen them. Your eyes are still there, perhaps. And your laugh. And that lurking smile, always ready to burst forth from your fantastically innocent face.

It was a beautiful day and I went and had a look outside. It might have happened then. I might have written to you just to say that then, that morning, I could have told you: could have said that, perhaps without realizing it, I loved you. You'd have been standing there, listening. I'd also have said that after that morning it would be too late: too late to tell you I loved you, and forever. That never again would I feel as intense a need to tell you so as in that grand apartment building on a northern beach, under a midday sky of wind and rain.

And then the sun came back again, green and harsh. And the weather turned cold.

The next day. In the morning.

The gulls approached up the sands, came close to the child and the girl.

And again, in the child's eyes, there was the faint fear of life.

Suddenly, heaven knows why, all the gulls flew out to sea together, borne by the wind, their feathers smoothed by it, white and pure as doves.

And then, far out at sea, and all together still, they wheeled slowly around and headed back for the beach. But this time they were caught up in gusts, the flock was tattered and torn, the gulls became raucous, wild, vulgar, brazen as human beings. The boy laughed. And so did the girl.

As the boy laughed he noticed how long the gulls were taking to get back to their realm of sand. And the fear came back into his eyes again, fear that they might not make it, that they might drown. But they did make it. Here they were. Dazed. Exhausted. But alive. "They really are cracked," the girl said. And the boy laughed.

After that the gulls rested for a while, and then they preened their feathers with their yellow beaks, and after that they howled again like dogs, like horses, you had to stop your ears. They were watching the sky and, above all, the confused swirling of the rain, which they alone could decipher. And already you could see the sand beginning to quiver as the blood-red sand-worms started climbing up toward the light.

The child watched the gulls swallow the long blood-red worms. He smiled at them. Sometimes one of the gulls would choke on a worm, and that made him laugh.

Yes. One day it will happen, one day you'll miss horribly what you described as "unbearable"—what we tried to do, you and I, in the summer of 1980, that summer of wind and rain.

Sometimes it happens by the sea. When the beach grows empty, at nightfall. After the children's summer camps have gone. All over the sands a shriek goes up, saying that Capri is over. *It was the city of our early love,* but now it's over. *Over.*

It's suddenly awful. Awful. Whenever it happens it makes you want to weep, run away, die, because Capri has revolved with the earth, revolved toward the forgetting of love.

There were no more bright intervals, it rained full time except during the night, which was lit up by clouds beneath a black sky. People were leaving. Rented houses and apartments were closed up. But the girls working as camp counselors, and the children's summer camps themselves, were still there. The children were still there in the blue tents tethered to piles of rocks. And in the tents they went on singing and telling stories. What songs they sang and what stories they told no one really knew, but the children went on listening. They'd have listened even if the stories were told in Chinese or Javanese or American. If you wanted to make them split their sides you sang songs in Chinese. Then they would all fall about and sing in "Chinese," and the girl counselors would laugh just as loudly as the children themselves.

Children who had parents and nice houses and cars came to see what was going on and why everyone was laughing so much, and then they started to laugh too and sang along with the children who were penniless.

Everybody was going home. Café terraces were windswept and empty. Streets were deserted. Visitors who stayed on played *boules* in empty sheds, or bridge in hotel lounges. Casinos stayed open day and night. Supermarkets were packed. Cafés were turning people away. They refused to serve whole families with cups of coffee. Not worth it. They'd say the coffee machine wasn't working, which as a matter of fact was true, because when it was raining they never served anything but strong drink. As for people with children, no problem, they didn't even let them in.

The summer camps had abandoned the beach. When it rained too much they just kept the kids shut away in their great dormitory village in the hills.

From the buildings up there the children could see the beach below stretching away into the distance, as well as others further away: the beach at Hennequeville and, better still, lower down, the rock fall from the cliffs overhanging the sea, an endless expanse of huge black stones that had tumbled down into the clay centuries ago, according to the camp counselors, or perhaps just a few nights back.

You asked me, "Where are we?"
I said, "At S. Thala."
"And after S. Thala?"
I said that after S. Thala it was S. Thala still. For that's where it is, the city of all love.

After that come the beaches at Villerville, said the girl—Agatha's beach. Beyond that again, Pennedepie and the black pales of the dukes of Alba. Beyond the estuary, she said, the Seine leaves the land behind and loses itself in the sea. There's still what was once a port for the African timber trade, and marshes swarming with eels and carp, and thickets full of young rabbits. And then the German factory, built of red brick and glass and now in ruins, facing the same river Seine as the one in Paris.

It's there that in one of my books you stand and

weep—there on the red ground glittering with shat-
tered glass, facing the river as it suddenly unleashes its
thousand horsepower and rushes into the ocean with
the speed of light.

And further off still, amid the alluvial soil of the
Vernier marshes, there's Quilleboeuf, where Emily L.
was seen by you and me for the first and last time in
her life.

The children were still there in the summer camps
provided for them by the local authorities on the hills
above the Résidence des Roches Noires. They'd been
told to put on their sweaters because of the rain and
the damp, the kind of weather that makes children
catch cold. And then they'd been made to sing. But
they didn't sing for long. Most of them just lay down
and went to sleep, and no one disturbed them. Most
of the girls, the camp counselors, fell asleep on the
ground, like the children.

Really, how could anyone resist such a thing—someone so childlike he wanted everything, and all at once. To tear books to pieces and burn them. And who was afraid on their behalf at their destruction. You knew the book already existed. You used to say, "What do you think you're doing? What's the point? Spending your whole time writing, all day and every day? Everybody will desert you—you're crazy, unbearable to live with. A nut. . . . You don't even notice that every table in the house is covered with heaps of your notes . . ."

Sometimes we laughed together over your sudden rages. Sometimes you were afraid I might throw the book in the sea, or burn it. Occasionally you came back at five in the morning from one of your rallies or a session spent contemplating the ineffable barmen who worked in the big hotels on the hill, supposed to be the most luxurious in the world. Often I was asleep when you came in. I'd hear you go into the main room to check if the manuscript was still there on the table and then into the kitchen to see if there was any coffee left in the packet—any bread, any butter, any coffee!

I began not talking to you any more, I was happy just saying good morning. I left you alone. Bought steaks for you. Just saw you in the morning, coming out of your room unshaven in search of a black coffee, and laughed till I cried at how stuffy you looked and how you inspected everything.

You were terrible, I was often afraid of you. And the people we knew were afraid for me. It seemed to me you were more and more sincere, but it was too late for me, I couldn't stop you. Just as I'd never been able to stop being afraid of you. You didn't know you made me afraid you might be going to kill me. All my women friends and acquaintances were charmed by how gentle you are. You were my best visiting card. But your gentleness made *me* think of the death you must unknowingly dream of inflicting on me. Every night.

Sometimes I was afraid as soon as you woke up. Like all men every day, even if only for a few seconds, you became a woman-killer. It might happen any day. Sometimes you were as frightening as a lost hunter or an escaped criminal. And this made the people around me afraid for me sometimes. And for me it was always there—I was afraid of you. Every day, for a few brief moments you were not even aware of, I was afraid when you looked at me.

Sometimes just your look frightened me. Sometimes it was as if I'd never seen you before. I couldn't remember why you'd come to this popular seaside resort at such an awful time of the year, when it was so crowded you were even more alone than in the city you came from.

I sometimes told myself I'd never seen you before—perhaps so that I'd be able to kill you or turn you out...I didn't know. I knew so little about you it was terrifying. I'd no idea why you were there, what you'd come for, or what would become of you. The present was the only thing we ever talked about.

You probably couldn't remember what you were doing there either, living with a woman old already and crazy with writing.

Perhaps it was just the usual thing, maybe it happened all the time and it was nothing, you just came because you were desperate, just as you were every day of your life. Just as, some summers, at certain hours of the days and nights, for instance when the sun left the sky and entered the sea, entered the sea every night for ever, you couldn't help wanting to die. I knew all about that.

I saw us both as lost in the same kind of nature. Sometimes my heart goes out to people like us. Unstable, others call us—a bit touched. "They don't go to the movies any more, or to the theater, or to parties." Lefties, you see, what can you expect, they've forgotten how to behave, turn up their noses at Cannes and smart hotels in Morocco. And at the movies and the theater too, of course.

The wind had started up again. And the sky had gone dark again too.

Once more the sea was a vast expanse of rain as far as the eye could see.

Under an awning, by the wall, was the little boy. He was looking at the sea, not playing with the pebbles he'd picked up on the beach. He just clutched them in his fists. He was dressed in red. The girl was beside him. She looked at him, then at the rain, then at him again. The child's eyes were brighter than usual, and larger, and more terrifying, too, because of the blind vastness of what there was to see.

And one day, soon after that, I remember, the girl went into a big white tent and started to tell a story about the sea and a little boy. All the children looked at the sea.

"Once upon a time," said the girl, "once upon a time there was a little boy called David. He'd set out with his parents to sail around the world in a yacht called the *Admiral System*.

"And one day the sea got rough.

"It got so rough that the *Admiral System* went down with all hands, except for little David. And what do you think? A shark who happened to be passing by said, 'Hey, little boy, just climb up on my back.' And so the two of them set out together over the sea."

"Ooh," said the children.

The girl paused and then went on.

"The shark swam very fast along the surface of the sea," she said.

And then she stopped and went to sleep. The children shouted at her and she went on.

She told the story slowly and very well. She wanted the children to be quiet, and they were completely quiet.

"The shark was called Triantywoppitygong," she

said. "Remember that name or you won't understand anything."

Some of the children laughed at the name. Others laughed at the shark. Others again laughed at the girl.

The children all shouted the name together as best they could.

And the little boy who didn't speak much, was he listening to the girl telling the story about David? Who can say, but probably he was, he was a child who listened to everything. That evening it was almost as if he'd never listened to a story before. He looked at the girl, and all you could see in his gray eyes was that they were looking at the girl. But they were looking at her as they might have looked at the gulls or the sea, beyond the beaches, beyond the sea, beyond the wind, the sands and the clouds, beyond the raucous gulls and the slaughtered red worms. And the girl went on telling the story of David, David and the shark with the name he couldn't pronounce . . .

The sea was milky blue. There was no wind to carry away the story of David told by the girl. She was stretched out on a piece of canvas now, looking up at the sky, telling the story just as it came into her head, and laughing. And the children laughed too, and listened with all their ears.

The weather was so mild the flocks of swallows were back, wheeling over the beach, beautiful, made of gray velvet, as if fascinated by the children, the flesh of the children. This made the children laugh.

"The shark scolded David for crying," the girl went on. "He reminded David it was he who had swallowed David's father and mother, and it wasn't tactful of David to cry in front of him."

And suddenly the girl seemed to have fallen asleep. The children started to shout.

"Tell us the story or we'll box your ears!" they shouted.

"Then the island appeared," said the girl, laughing.

She said she'd forgotten, but now she remembered.

"'It's a tropical island!' cried David."

And then she said she'd forgotten what came next.

"Sorry," she said. "I forget."

Then the children yelled, "You can't, you can't!"

So she went on anyway. And the children listened as before, but then they noticed she wasn't telling the same story, the one she'd started before, and again they shouted, "Tell us the story or we'll box your ears!"

So she went on:

"'It's a tropical island!' cried David.

"'That's right,' said the shark."

Then she said she didn't know any more, really she didn't . . .

And she fell asleep.

It was the evening of a bright but sunless day. The girl from the summer camp was walking along the boardwalk. She was with the little boy. He walked a bit to one side of her. They were both walking slowly. She spoke to him. She told him she loved him. Loved a child.

She told him how old she was, eighteen, and her name. She asked him to repeat it. He repeated her name and age. "Johanna," he said. "Eighteen," he said. Then he said the name Johanna again. Then he asked, "Johanna what?" And the girl said, "Goldberg, Johanna Goldberg." And the boy repeated the whole of the name.

The girl asked him what his name was.

The boy said, "Steiner, Samuel."

And he smiled at an image that only he in the whole world could remember.

He said, "And my little sister's name was Steiner, Judith."

The boy and the girl counselor. They walked along together.

They were thin, slim, they both had the same body and the same slow, languid walk. That morning they were walking along by the sea. As thin and pale as one another. Babes in the wood . . .

The other female counselors and captains seemed to be growing uneasy. Because they were always together.

Under the streetlight she stopped, took the child's face in her hands and tilted it up to the light to look at his eyes.

"Gray," she said.

Then she let go of his face and spoke to him.

She told him he'd remember the summer of 1980 all his life. The summer when he was six. When he looked at everything. Including the stars. And the long line of tankers from Antifer. Everything. And she told him to look carefully tonight. At the sea, the town, the towns across the river, the revolving beams of the lighthouses. Look carefully at all the different ships at sea, the black oil tankers that were so beautiful. And the big English ferryboats, the white ships. . . . And all the fishing boats—"Look over there at all the lights"—and she told him to listen carefully too, to all the sounds of the night. She told him this was the summer when he was six. He would never be six again. And he must also take care to remember the rue de Londres—she and he were the only two people who knew about it—which was the Temple of the Sun. She said that in the year when he was sixteen, on the same day of the same month as today, he could come back, and she would be here on this same part of the beach, but later, about midnight. He said he didn't quite understand what she was saying, but he would come.

She said she'd recognize him, and he must wait for her opposite the rue de Londres. He couldn't miss it.

She said, "We'll make love to one another."

He said yes. He didn't say he didn't understand.

She said, "The sea will be deserted, it will be dark

by then and the beaches will be empty, too. All the people will be at home with their families."

They both walked toward the sea until they disappeared amid the sands, until they frightened the people watching them.

Until they reappeared, approaching the tennis courts.

She was carrying him on her shoulders. She was singing, the song about resting by the spring and never forgetting him.

They'd been walking a long time. It was late now, and the beaches were deserted.

They left the boardwalk behind and disappeared into the hills.

After they'd gone it was still not quite dark. He said he wanted to tell her something.

Then the girl wept again and said there was no need, she knew what he'd have liked to tell her but there was no need, she knew, the people at the orphanage had told her. And then she hid her face and wept and told the rest of the story about David.

The other children always gathered round when the counselors told stories.

"So," said the girl, "here we are on the tropical island. Triantywoppitygong dropped David on a beach. 'Here you are on Fountain Island,' he told him. David asked where the Fountain was. The shark said she lived in a big iron cage. David thanked the shark. 'Thanks, Mr. Shark,' he said. 'Don't mention it,' said the shark, 'but what are you going to do?' 'I'll think of something,' said David. 'But what about you? What are you going to do?' 'Nothing, the same as you,' said the shark. Then he said he was going to Guatemala, as a matter of fact. What else? David approved. 'A drop of warm seawater in winter is good for chronic bronchitis,' said the shark. And he began to stare at David. And seeing him so fresh and plump, the shark had a nervous breakdown and started to shout and gibber all anyhow, grunting and gurgling and bawling and gnashing his teeth and so on. So David told him to calm down. 'All right,' said the shark, and did calm down."

Then the children asked the girl to talk "all anyhow." She said she couldn't, it was too difficult.

"So David and the shark parted. They wished each

other bon voyage and good health and a happy New Year, and went their separate ways. What else could they do?

"After the shark had gone, David went to sleep and then woke up, and then went to sleep again, and so on and so forth for some time. And then one evening something happened. The sky went dark as night and as stormy and gold as the color of the sea, and it all happened too fast for anyone to understand what was going on."

And suddenly, instead of continuing with the story, the girl lay down on the sand and said she felt sleepy. So the children shouted and boxed her ears and called her names, and she only laughed. "Are you going on with the story or not? If you don't, we'll kill you." And she still went on laughing. She fell asleep laughing, and they went for a swim in the sea. Except the boy with gray eyes. He stayed by her sleeping body.

One morning the sky was lacquer blue and the sun still behind the hills. The boy went along the boardwalk. I watched him. Watched him till he disappeared. Then shut my eyes to see that vast gray gaze again.

The girl stood still on the boardwalk and watched the boy coming back. Here he was. He was looking at the postcard she'd told him to buy. He knew the best ones were to be found in the general store. She'd told him so. He'd done as she'd told him.

The girl wrote something on the postcard.

And now on the back of the postcard there was the girl's name, the date—July 30, 1980—and the date and time he was to come back ten years hence—July 30, 1990, at midnight.

On the front of the postcard there was a picture of where they'd been the previous evening—the place where the road to the tennis courts met the prome-

nade and the rue de Londres—the most beautiful
street of all, she said, her favorite, lovely as a tunnel of
sunlight against the sea.

In the sea, as in sleep, I couldn't tell the boy from
the other children. I could see him, though, when she
came over to him. I looked at them both. The tide
was out. The sun was huge, stretching from one hori-
zon to the other, yellow as gold.

That was when it happened, she came over to him
and I saw. She lifted him on to her shoulders and they
moved forward into the sea as if to die together. But
no. The boy was just letting her coax him into the sea.
He was still a bit frightened, though his fear made
him shout with laughter.

They came out of the sea. She dried him, dried his
body. Then left him and went back in. He watched
her. She waded right out. At low tide you had to walk

out a long way to reach deep water. The boy didn't take his eyes off her. He was always scared when she went a long way out, but he didn't say anything. She lay on the water and started to swim. Scarcely turning around to blow a kiss in his direction. And then he couldn't see her any more, she was swimming out to sea, her head bent into the waves. He went on watching her. Around her the sea was forgotten by the wind, and she was abandoned by her own strength, graceful as a woman deep asleep.

The boy sat down.

Still watching her.

The girl came back. She always did. Then she asked him if he remembered her name, the name she'd written on the postcard. He said a name and a surname. She said that was right, that was her name.

The girl went to sleep.

The boy gazed at the beach, not quite understanding how it came to be there and why he'd never seen it before. Then he stopped trying to understand and moved over beside the girl. She was asleep. He slid his hand gently under hers so she shouldn't forget him. Her hand didn't move. And then the boy went straight to sleep too.

Then, the next day, the sun came back again. When no one expected it any more, there it was again in a perfect sky. Below, the sea was as calm and innocent and smooth as the sky. You could see beyond Le Havre and Sainte-Adresse and even Antifer.

From the dark room we looked out at the brightness and transparency of the night. You were beside me. I said, "Someone, some day, must describe how beautiful Antifer is. Say how it's simultaneously alone and with God. Wild and bare along the primeval cliffs, commensurate with the absolute absence of a possibility of God."

The girl came back from swimming in the sea. She was naked, too, like the boy, and her body was now stretched out beside his.

They lay for a long time silent, eyes shut.

And then she went on telling him the story about the shark.

"That night, the color of storm and gold," she said, "David heard a sound, a living sound—someone on the island was crying, but not angrily, perhaps unconsciously, perhaps in their sleep.

"David went to look, and when he turned around he saw all the animals on the island lying down in the golden light. A great tawny expanse dotted with the diamonds of their eyes. Eyes all looking at him.

"'Don't be frightened,' cried David. 'I'm the lost child.'

"Then the animals all came up to him.

"'Who is it that's crying?' he asked.

"'The Fountain,' said the animals.

"And from the sea, blown on the wind, came the sound of gentle tears.

"'She weeps every night. She's a weeping Fountain. She comes from a faraway country called Guatemala, and to get here she has to cross two oceans and twenty-two submarine continents.'

"'And she's seven hundred million years old,' said an old hare, 'and now she's had enough and wants to die, and at night she calls out for death.'

"David didn't answer.

"'So that's why she's crying, you see,' said a very small panther.

"'You have to see it from her point of view,' said a little gray monkey.

"'I think she may be listening,' said David.

"'Someone's calling out—listen! It's the Fountain, the mother of us all, the Great Mestiza of the oceans. The great tropical Fountain of the northern world,' said the little white monkey.

"All the animals listened. David too.

"'Who is it that has come to the island?' asked the Fountain in a tiny voice.

"'A boy,' said the young Asian buffalo.

"'Oh, a young human . . .'

"'That's right.'

"'Has he got hands?' asked the Fountain.

"'Yes,' answered all the animals together. 'At least two hands, apparently. . .'

"David showed the animals and the Fountain his hands.

"'He's picking up a stone,' said the animals.

"'He's throwing it up in the air.'

"'He's catching it.'

"'Was it him playing the harmonica this evening then?' asked the Fountain.

"'Yes, tonight it was him,' said the animals. They were glad for the Fountain's sake. Before, they hadn't known who young David was, but tonight he was clearly the one playing the harmonica.

"'God be thanked,' said the Fountain. 'And young David, too.'

"'Yes,' echoed the animals.

"The Fountain said a prayer in some extraordinary gobbledygook. The animals, each supplying his own particular response, produced a most curious racket.

"Then, 'And does this boy know how to kill?' asked the Fountain slyly.

"'No,' said the animals. Then they all waited. They knew the Fountain would clutch at anything in order to die, and they meant to prevent it.

"'No, certainly not,' they said. 'This boy wouldn't kill anything.'

"The Fountain fell silent. For a long time. And then all of a sudden, through the peaceful darkness, they could hear a great rushing of water.

"'She's emerging from the cistern of the Atlantic,' said the animals.

"And then the Fountain actually appeared."

The girl said the Fountain was at the same time a person and a mountain of water, glassy as emerald. She had no arms, no face, she was blind, and moved without motion so as not to spoil the pleats in her aqueous draperies.

"She was searching for David's hands," said the girl.

"The setting sun entered the Fountain's dead eyes, and then night fell.

"'David, David,' called the blind Fountain.

"She was trying to find David so that she might die. And the boy looked all around him.

"The Fountain wept. 'David, David,' she cried.

"So this is what David did. He got out his harmonica and played an ancient polka from Guatemala.

"And then . . . and then . . . listen carefully . . . then the Fountain paused in amazement, and slowly, but with a youthful, childlike grace, started to dance the charming leisurely polka from her native country.

"She danced till dawn," said the girl, "and when day came she went on dancing in her sleep. Then the animals on the island led her gently back into the dark cave of the Atlantic. They warmed her shadowy body with kisses, and the kisses brought her back to life. Brought her back to life through the forgetting of life."

The girl fell silent. The boy with gray eyes had lain down beside her and gone to sleep. But he put his hands on the girl's young breasts. She didn't move, didn't stop him. He found her breasts under her dress. His hands were cold because of the sea wind. He marveled. He held her breasts tight, so tight that it hurt, but he couldn't let them go, couldn't forget them, and when she put his hands away his eyes filled with tears.

We talked of things that had nothing to do with the events of the afternoon or the coming night, but that did relate to God and the so-present absence of God. Things like the breasts of the girl, who was so young to be confronted by the coming immensity.

Callas voiced her despair one last time, and Capri descended to kill her. And once Norma was slain, the shrieks of "Capri is over" reigned supreme over beaches, countries, cities and oceans, and the shattering fact was confirmed that this was the end of the world.

August 1980.

There I was by that crowded beach, with the sun revolving around the circle of the sky.

August 1980. Gdansk.

The port of Gdansk. Now a universal symbol for the suffering of countries invaded because they were poor and alone.

Gdansk, which made me tremble like the boy. Alone like him. A prisoner. Strangled by the endemic fascism of central Germany.

The boy went by, together with the other children from the camp. He turned and looked behind him, and then looked at the sea.

The girl arrived later bringing breakfast. She went up to the boy and put an arm around his neck. She spoke to him. He glanced up at her as he walked along, listening closely, smiling sometimes. Like her. She seemed happy—because of Gdansk, she said. He didn't know anything about Gdansk, but he was glad too.

She told him how the shark used to come to the island to see David. Sometimes he would speak with an American accent, sometimes with a Spanish one, and at another time with no accent at all, just a sneezing and snuffling and roaring that had to be put up with. The boy laughed. Roared with laughter. The girl paused while he laughed, then went on with the story. One day, she said, the shark came wearing a baseball cap that he'd found in the sewers of New York on his way to a rock concert. No one knew where the concert was, nor if it really was a concert, such a racket, but that was the shark all over, nothing to be done about it, he was stupid, said the girl. Stupido.

The boy asked what the shark was doing in New York.

The girl said the shark was acting on behalf of the shoals of herring and went to the ports of New York and Mandalay to spy on the fishermen and report back to the herrings. "Not very nice," said the girl, "but that's life." The boy didn't seem to understand.

Then she said that one day when the shark came back to the island he asked David to go away with him. He wanted to show him the Sargasso Sea, where there was never any wind, where there were never any waves, only a long, gentle swell. And never any cold. And sometimes the sea turned white with the milk of a mother whale wounded in the dugs, and people bathed in the milky sea, and drank it, and wallowed in its warmth. A pleasure beyond description.

"'Come, David. Come! David!'

"And in the end, David said he'd go.

"Then the shark wept, and David didn't know why.

"And all the animals on the island gathered around David and started to perform their evening toilet, and they licked David too. So he was their child now.

"But the shark wanted to come up on to the sand and steal David away. There was no stopping him. But the animals said, 'Don't be afraid—we're here.'

"And David said to the shark, 'There you go again—no one can ever understand what you want.'

"And the shark wept and kept bawling out that it wasn't his fault.

"So David started weeping with him, about the unjust fate meted out to sharks.

"And suddenly the light brightened and the air echoed with liquid thunder, and the Great Mestiza of all the oceans slowly emerged from the cistern of the Atlantic to see the sunset.

"Still blind, but very beautiful, the Fountain asked who was howling, she said it was disgraceful, you couldn't hear yourself speak down in the cistern of the Atlantic.

"And then all the animals said together, 'It's the shark—he wants to eat David.' Then David understood, and felt sorry for the shark.

"'They're all completely nuts on this island,' said the Great Mestiza. She said it in French."

The boy asked if the Fountain always danced in

the evening. The girl said yes, every evening until it was dark, and not always in time to the music, nor always to the polka from Guatemala, sometimes to a tango by Carlos d'Alessio. And sometimes to the slow Funeral Passacaglia, no one in those parts was sure who wrote it, though according to one school of thought he was probably some old German organist.

The boy asked how long David stayed on the island. The girl said two years. But she wasn't sure either.

Then she asked him if he wanted to know the end of the story. He shook his head. He didn't want to. He didn't say any more. He started to cry. He didn't want the Fountain to die, nor the shark either.

"Nor David?" asked the girl.

"Nor David," he said.

And then the girl asked the boy another question. She asked him what he would have preferred David to do—kill the Fountain or let her stay alive.

The boy looked at the sea and the sands without seeing them. He hesitated, then said, "I'd rather he killed her."

And then he asked, "What about you?"

She said she didn't know. But perhaps she'd rather the Fountain was killed, too.

She said people didn't know why they wanted the Fountain to die.

The boy said no, they didn't.

Suddenly, beyond the windowpanes, it was night. Night which had fallen unnoticed and was already very dark. And we thought about the cruelty of the boy and of the sea and about all the things that are so different and yet so alike.

The girl said people were always writing books on the end of the world and the death of love. But she saw that the boy didn't understand. And this made them both laugh, made them both roar with laughter. He said it wasn't true—people wrote books on paper.

Marguerite Duras

They laughed. And then she said the boy did understand. They laughed again. And she said if love and
the sea didn't exist, no one would write any books
at all.

The summer camps had come through the summer. The boy with gray eyes was still there. And with him, always, the girl. Everyone sang songs, except them—the boy and the camp counselor. The boy and the lone girl.

So then they went out beyond the jetty again. To the mounds of clay and the black stakes. And there she sang for the boy about how she'd gone again and again to the clear spring. That's what she sang. She said it was the song the non-Jewish deportees sang when they were being held at Rambouillet. He asked who the deportees were.

She said, "Frenchmen." And then she said that later on the Jewish deportees sang the same song, the song about the clear spring, before they died.

Then she didn't say any more for a long time.

And then she said they were all Jews.

The tide was going out, and the girl told the boy about a book she'd read lately, it still preoccupied her, she couldn't get it out of her head. It was about a love that awaited death without actually provoking it, a love infinitely more intense than if it had acted through desire.

The girl told the child that what he didn't understand about what she said was like what she didn't understand about herself when she looked at him. She told him she loved him. She said, "I love you more than anything else in the world."

The boy wept.

The girl didn't ask why.

Then the boy wanted to know more about the Jews. The girl didn't know.

As on the first day, the sea drove the white swathes of its wrath up on to the beach, then took them back again as it might a past love. . . . Or the ashes of the Jews burned in the German crematoria, who will never be forgotten until the end of all the centuries the world has left to live.

The boy with gray eyes stood there. So did the girl. Like strangers.

They looked at the sea to avoid looking at one another. Trying not to see one another ever again. Not to speak to one another ever again.

And while they were looking at something else, the boy wept.

And I brought them both back, as I do you, out of the sea and the wind, and shut them up in this dark room lost in a dimension above time. What I call the Room of the Jews. My room. And the room of Yann Andrea Steiner.

The boy wept for some time. The girl let him weep. He'd forgotten about her.

And then she asked, "What is it you're remembering...?"

The boy said, "Nothing." And then he was silent. And then he said quite clearly that the German soldier had shot his little sister in the head and her head had exploded. The boy wasn't crying now. He was trying to remember, and he *was* remembering. He said there was blood everywhere. And the dog too, the German soldier killed the dog too, because it went for him. The way the dog howled...he said he could still remember that.

Two years old his little sister was. He couldn't remember anything else.

He fell silent. He looked at the girl. He turned pale. He was afraid of saying something he wanted to hide. He said he couldn't remember.

The girl said nothing. She looked at him again. She said, "Yes. One can't remember anything."

He said yes, except for his little sister Judith, he couldn't remember anything.

He was silent. Then he said, "My mother shouted

to me to run away, to get away as fast as I could, straight away, and not tell anybody about Judith ever. Not ever."

The boy stopped suddenly. As if he was going out of his mind. As if fear was suddenly supreme again, as if he'd suddenly started to be afraid of her, the girl, too.

She looked at him for a while and then said, "You must talk about it. Otherwise we'll both die."

She could see he didn't understand. She said that otherwise it would all happen again.

The boy looked at her again and smiled and said, "You were joking . . ."

She smiled back. He asked, "Are you a Jew too?"

She said yes, she was a Jew too.

The boy had never seen such a storm before. He was probably scared. So the girl picked him up in her arms and they went out into the foam together.

The boy was terrified. He'd forgotten the girl.

And it was while he'd forgotten her that the girl saw his gray eyes in the full force of their light. Then she shut her own eyes, and stopped herself from advancing further into the deep foam, as she'd have liked to do, to kill them, too, these other two Jews, herself and him.

The boy was still looking at the waves, their coming and going. His body had stopped trembling.

The girl, her face averted from the sea, kissed the boy's hair, it smelled like the wind from the sea, and she wept, and that evening the boy knew why.

She asked the boy if he was cold, and he said he wasn't. And if he was still frightened, and he said no, but he was lying. He corrected himself. He said, "I am sometimes. At night."

He asked her if she couldn't go out further, to where the waves broke, and she said if she did the force of the sea would probably separate them and sweep him away. He laughed at this as if it were a joke.

She asked him about his parents. The boy didn't know where they were buried. He said they'd taken pills, as his mother had always told him they would. She'd turned him out of the house, and they must have died directly afterwards.

Had he seen them dead?

No. Only his little sister and the dog.

Had he seen the German soldiers?

No. But on the road, after he'd left, some drove past in a car.

The girl was weeping piteously now, but in silence. He looked at her. He was amazed. But he didn't say anything.

"And what happened to you afterwards? What can you remember?"

"I started walking along the road. And in a field there were some horses and a woman who'd heard the gunshots. She called me over and gave me some bread and some milk. I stayed with her in her house, but she was afraid of the Germans so she hid me.

"And then she got frightened again and sent me to the orphanage."

"And have you been there all the time?"

"I think so. On Sundays we used to go into the forest. I remember that."

"Didn't you ever go to the sea?"

"No. This is the first time."

She said, "Do you like it in the orphanage?"

He said yes, he did. But he wept. And he spoke again and said, crying out this time, "When the

German soldier shot my sister the dog went for him and the soldier killed the dog too."

They looked at one another again. He said, "I can remember that very clearly—the dog barking."

Then he didn't look any more. He stared into space. He said his mother had told him they were Jews. And the Germans were killing the Jews, all of them. The Germans wanted there not to be any Jews any more, ever.

He hesitated, then asked if it was still going on, if the Germans were killing people still.

The girl said no. He looked at her. She didn't know if he believed her.

Afterwards they walked on northward, in the direction of the marshes around the bay of the Seine, before the jetties in the harbor.

They went across the now exposed sands and

toward the Black Stakes and the canal. The hollows in the beach were muddy here, and the girl carried the boy again.

They crossed the bay, with its great expanse of sand. The stakes grew taller as they approached them.

And then the girl put the boy down, and they went on as far as the last sandbank before the Seine, the river she called it, which went on flowing into the sea and then disappeared. She told him to look at the color of the water, to see where it was green and where it was blue.

He looked.

The girl lay down on the sand and shut her eyes.

Then the boy went over to the people gathering shellfish nearby. When he'd gone she wept.

From time to time he came back to her.

She knew when he was standing there looking at her.

She knew both when he went back to the fishermen and when he came back to her again.

He gave her what the fishermen had left behind,

little gray crabs, shrimps, empty shells. And she threw them into the pool of water at the foot of the tallest black stake.

And then, slowly, the sea took on a sheen of pearly green.

And the long line of tankers from Antifer grew darker.

And the waters of the Seine began to be invaded by the waters of the sea. And the difference between the waters of the Seine and the waters of the sea was plain. Like an open book.

The boy came back to the girl. He cuddled up close to her and they gazed at one another for a long time. She especially. As if he were a stranger all of a sudden.

And she said, "You are the boy with gray eyes, that's what you are."

He saw she'd been crying while he was away. He said he didn't like it when she cried. He knew it was because of his little sister, but sometimes he couldn't help it, couldn't help talking about Maria. She asked him what color Maria's eyes were. He couldn't remember. Green, he thought. That was what his mother said.

Time passed. Soon it would be autumn. But they hadn't yet reached the end of the summer.

Suddenly it grew cold.

The girl carried the little boy, holding him tight, embracing his body. And he said that sometimes at night he dreamed he was still weeping for his little sister, and for the dog.

He looked at the canal, perhaps he was scared because they were alone now in that great stretch of sand. The girl told him not to be frightened any more. She put him down, and he wasn't afraid any more, and they walked back the way they had come, along the path between fields left uncultivated because they were flooded by the sea at high tide.

Then the girl talked to him. Told him she'd rather things stayed as they were between them.

She'd rather the story ended there, even if the boy didn't understand it, rather it ended in this desire as it was now, even though it might lead her to kill herself. It wouldn't be a real death, of course—a dead death, rather, where you don't feel any pain, you're not sad, you're not punished or anything.

She said, "I want it to be quite impossible."

She said, "I want it to be quite desperate."

She said that if he'd been older the story would have gone away and left them, she couldn't even imagine such a thing, it was best for it to be as it was between them. She said that if he didn't understand all she was saying it didn't matter. The boy wept, wept he didn't know why, as if the killing of his little sister had never ended and were still slowly spreading over all the earth.

And she said she knew he couldn't understand what she was saying to him yet, but the knowledge wasn't enough to stop her saying it.

The boy listened to it all. He listened to everything, that child.

As they went along he looked at her sometimes, gazed as if seeing her for the first time.

At first he didn't say anything. Anything at all.

Then he said he was tired and asked her to carry him again. When she'd picked him up he gazed into her face with a seriousness she'd never seen before, and he suddenly said, very quietly, as if he might be overheard, that if she didn't take him with her he'd jump into the sea and drown. The other children had told him how you went about it, so he knew what to do.

So then the girl promised to take him with her whatever happened, swore to him that she'd never never leave him, never never forget him.

The end had begun.

The children from the southern suburbs came and waited around the buses, watched over by the drivers.

The woman in charge of the camp for children from the southern suburbs looked over toward the hill.

She said, "We'll have to notify the police. The boy still isn't back. Nor is the counselor."

They'd have to sound the alarm.

A call went up from the Touques estuary. A sound like a siren signalling the end of the day at one of those little factories you see by the roadside.

The girl lay down behind a bush. The boy came and lay close by, as if he was trying to lose himself, disappear inside her. He didn't understand. It was frightening. He cried out, "I'm going to stay with you."

Another call went up, slower, not so loud. She said, "You go. I'll follow."

Then the boy stood up and looked. Looked at the tennis courts in the distance, at the locked-up villas, and at her, lying there weak and speechless, and he looked at the buses in the distance, and the trucks, waiting to go back to the southern suburbs. And then he looked up at the hills. There it was all quite peaceful. It was all quite clear. The boy must have known already what he must do so as never to return.

A third call, longer, louder, died away over the sea. The girl cried out faintly, "Go now. *Please!*"

The boy took one more look at the great desert of summer and at her, this stranger.

And he said, "Come with me."

She said no, not now. She'd wait and join him later. But she would come. Tonight, she said, or tomorrow, or later still, but not this evening—this evening she didn't feel she ought to, she said. They must wait a bit longer, she said. He did as she'd asked. Slowly he moved away and started walking. And then he headed toward the hill.

She didn't watch him go. She started to sing again, sang about how she'd gone and rested beside the clear spring.

And she rested now, stretched out at full length, her eyes shut. And she sang joyfully, boldly.

As soon as she started to sing the boy stopped being afraid.

They looked at one another and suddenly laughed, a peal of joy. And the boy understood: she never would forget him now, never again, and the crime against the Jews had vanished from the earth with the knowledge of his and her story.

In the dark room, time suddenly subsided. And it was evening.

She told him she would take him with her wherever she went. That she'd be back with him tonight, but he must start out and walk till he reached to the forest, and then he must follow the paths marked out in white for foreign tourists.

I remember something.

It happened at the beginning. And yet I've only just started to remember.

She asked him, "What do you like most?"

He tried to understand the question and then asked her, what did she like most? She answered, "The same as you—the sea."

And he said yes, the sea.

I didn't know anything any more about the differences between the outside and the inside of the boy, between that which was all around him and kept him alive, and that which separated him from life, this masquerade of a life, separated him from it endlessly.

Then I came back to the fragility of his childish body, the temporary differences, the light beats of his heart showing his life advancing day and night toward an unknown future destined for him alone.

Nor did I know anything any more about the difference between the men of Gdansk and the men of God. Between the thousands of children who starved to death in Vilna, and the young priest Jerzy Popieluszko.

Nor about the difference between the graves in the East, and the poems buried in the ground in Silesia and the Ukraine. Between the deathly silence of Afghanistan, and the bottomless malevolence of the aforementioned God.

I didn't know anything any more. Anything about anything. Anywhere. Except the truth of the truth and the untruth of lies. I could no longer tell the difference between words and tears. All I knew was that the boy was walking along the path through the forest.

Walking. Alone. But still walking.

Still walking. And I knew that the girl, the counselor, had stood up, and that she was looking through the trees and could see his red sweater. And she called out a word in a low voice, and the boy recognized it and called it out too. A word that can't be written, that can be said only between Jews, and this has been so for ten thousand years, a hundred thousand, who can say?

I pressed my lips to Gdansk and kissed that Jewish child and the dead children of the Vilna ghetto. I embraced them too in my mind and in my body.

You say, "What did we talk about in the dark room?"

I say that like you I don't know any more.

About the events of the summer no doubt, the rain, hunger.

Injustice.

And death.

And bad weather, and the hot nights flowing into the August days, and the cool shade of walls,

and the cruel girls so lavish of desire,

and the endless hotels, now put a stop to,

and the cool dark corridors, the now-deserted rooms where so many books were written and so much love made,

and the man at Cabourg, Jewish like the boy, and what he wrote, Jewish as his soul,

and those long evenings, remember?, when they danced for him, the two naughty girls, for him, tortured by desire for them almost to the point of death, and lying there weeping on the sofa in the big drawing room overlooking the sea,

in the wild ecstasy of hoping to die of it some day, one day,

and Mozart and the blue of midnight on Arctic lakes,

and the blue light of midnight on voices singing in casinos of snow and frost—enough to make your heart tremble. Yes, voices singing tunes by Mozart, and murdered Jews, and also the way you had of doing nothing, and the way I had of waiting for you to come down to the beach. To see. See your eyes, laughing, more and more every day,

and your way of waiting too, on divans looking outward, on far continents, on oceans, on sorrow, on joy,

and about that child, on and on endlessly. And about his living for ever.

We talked about Poland. A Poland of the future, ablaze with hope and the idea of God,

and the postcard the boy brought back for the girl,

and again of Poland, homeland of us all, and of the living dead of Vilna, and of the Jewish children,

and the rue de Londres, so strangely beautiful, smooth, bare of all detail, naked as a look.

The boy went on walking. On and on. We couldn't see him any more.

We stayed apart from one another.

I closed my eyes. Stood with my closed eyes turned toward the hill.

You looked *for* me.

You said the buses carrying the first batch of children had set off along the main road. You said it was raining, but it was still summer rain, light and warm.

You said, "The boy has gone past the hill." You shouted, "But where's he going?"

You said, "She hasn't looked at him." I understood: she was leaving him to blaze the trail. She would follow in his footsteps, letting him do as he pleased as if he were fate.

I asked if you hoped you'd never see them again, never see any trace of their passing or of their bodies.

You didn't answer.

You said, "The boy's still walking."

I said he wouldn't die. I swore it. I wept, I shouted, I swore by the boy's own life.

You said he was disappearing, hiding, and she couldn't see him any more.

You said it was over: he'd disappeared, but not to die, never again to die, never, never. And you shouted with fear.

I shouted that I loved you. You didn't hear. From fear, from hope, you were still shouting too.

You said that now, even if she wanted to, she couldn't see him. I said, "She couldn't kill herself either."

You said you could see the boy again, he'd gone up the hill, he was hidden by the trees, he hadn't gone over to the buses. He must have hesitated, then made up his mind. He hadn't gone over to the buses. It was raining.

You said he would never go over to the buses now, never in all his life, and we wept with joy.

He'd done as she'd told him.

You said, "She told him last night to go up the hill overlooking the parking lot. He went quite openly past the parking lot where the buses were. Some of the truck drivers saw him and blew him kisses without looking at him, just looking down toward the sea. Then he was scared again and at first he walked faster, then he smiled back at the truck drivers."

And suddenly the light subsided, and so did time, and dusk swept through the forest and over the sea.

The boy went on walking.
He didn't wait for her. He knew she'd come.
He went on.
And she stood up. When she started out she was some way behind him. Then she grew closer. And came to the hill.
Every so often she was so near him he could hear her footsteps, and he smiled and wept at one and the same time, wept tears of wildest joy.

In the dark room we stayed apart from one another.
I kept my eyes closed. But looked at them, saw them. Wept for their happiness.
We couldn't share that joy. We didn't want to. We could only weep for it.
You went on describing how they made their way over the hill.
You said, "They must have reached the other side.

She's close behind him." You said, "They're in a state of terror-struck joy."

You said, "He hasn't looked back. She doesn't want to join him yet. She's as white as chalk. She's afraid. But she's laughing. She's so young, yet at the same time half dead. She knows that."

I asked you if you hoped you'd see them again some time, in some city street, who knows?

You said yes, you hoped for that more than you'd ever hoped for anything else.

You said, "They're on the point of leaving us."

You said it was over.

You said, "Now, even if she wanted to, she couldn't stay on the hill any longer, she'd be arrested as soon as it got dark. She'll have to go with the boy."

And now she sang to the boy, sang very softly about how she had rested by the clear spring, and how she would never never forget him and never leave him. Never, never, never.

We were back in the hotel at Roches Noires.

We went out on to the balcony. We didn't say anything.

We wept. We still do.

More children from the southern suburbs arrived early in the evening. It was still light. They called out the names of the newcomers. Some of the children had the same names as before. There was another Samuel.

And I wept again.

And then you didn't say any more, about either the boy or the girl. You talked about the woman, Theodora Kats. You asked again why I hadn't written any more about her.

You wanted to understand that about me, only that.

I said I'd been able to talk about her until I found out about that hotel in the Swiss Alps. And there the book stopped.

I said she was too much for a book. Much too much.

You said, "Or perhaps too little."

Perhaps Theodora couldn't be made into a book.

Perhaps it was too much, that white, that patience, that strange inexplicable waiting. And that indifference. Writing came to an end with her name. Her name alone was all the writing there could be about Theodora Kats. The name said it all.

That, and the white of her dresses and of her skin.

Perhaps Theodora Kats was something as yet unknown. An unknown enjoining on writing another silence. The silence imposed by women and by Jews.